MATFILS DIARY: INTO THE WILDERNESS

A NOVELLA

ANMOL RAI SAMSUHANG

Made with ♥ on the Notion Press Platform
www.notionpress.com

Dedicated to my grandparents

Lt. Krishna Das Rai Samsuhang,

our holy Koppa.

Lt. Indra Shova Rai Samsuhang,

our holy Koku.

Contents

Preface

This work is my first attempt to write a novel in English language, and with the successful status of my previous book made me more encouraged to write. And this time I thought of working on a novel, so with my avid enthusiasm and hard work

I am able to present you all my new work in literature. If I have to talk about becoming a novelist is that I drew all the interest and inspiration from one of the most prolific Indian writer R.K Narayan.

As a student its hard to manage time for following up your hobbies, but if you believe in yourself and work hard, you will definitely be kissed by success. And as it goes with the saying of Swami Vivekananda 'Everything is easy,

When you are busy.

But nothing is easy,

When you're lazy....

So till the last keep working are follow what you like to do, that enhances your capabilities and make you realize your true potential. And in this book also, you will get to read about the struggle of a man with the inevitable extremities.

As you go through the pages you get to know the serenity of this novel.

Enjoy reading

Anmol Rai Samsuhang

31st January 2023, Kolakham

Acknowledgements

First of all, I would like to express my flowing gratitude to the 'Notion Press' organization and to every member of it who showed their embroilment for the publication of this book.

Secondly to my family, relatives and friends for guiding me up in this sucessful publication

of my book. And special sense of gratitude to my teachers for all your fruitful knowledge and support

Prologue

Firstly, I would like to state that this is a fictional story about a boy named Emmanuel who finds his passion as an ecologist

which eventually turns into a revolutionary character and manages to save the wilderness from mass extinction.

There is a frequent mentioning or we can find the whole story in a country called Matfills and a village, Bulhort, which are the fictional places created by the novelist himself. Now the readers are going to be taken to the visionary world in an

adventure with the writer.

Through the pages we will jump into different characters that will give you mixed emotions of their role in the story.

I personally say that this novel portraits the current situation in which we all are living, where the wilderness is experiencing cruelty that the humans are causing around.

So, I would like to convey with the emotions and thought of the people reding this book in every chapter we pass on. Lastly I would like to add that if we all work together to save our planet we will be able to make a better place for the future generations and trust me there will be no need of setting our livelihood on mars. Respectfully,

Anmol Rai Samsuhang

CHAPTER ONE

BEGINNING

Eleven-year-old Emmanuel sitting on a bench is enjoying the ambiance of the setting sun and the alluring nature which he loves. He was born into a wealthy family to Mrs. Victoria Green and Mr. David Green in the small village of Bulhort, Matfils. Mr. Green is a politician and Mrs. Green is the owner of eleven parlors.

Immanuel is now in his last years at the Matfils high school.

"Immanuel where are you? Mrs. Green is seen wailing.

Immanuel hears this, who is enjoying the evening glimpse of setting sun from above his house. He rushes down to his mother who is in her top voice.

'Immanuel where were you gone, dear?

"Not so far, just above there"

"Your father has brought you a gift, go check it"

He gets to know that his father has brought him a gift, and he is very curious to find it out. Mr. Green calls him to the dinning hall and bangs a giant box on the table. Immanuel hurriedly unboxes everything and gets to know that it is a book. He becomes elated to find out that it is a book and since age seven he is fond of reading books, so getting a book as a gift was immense pleasure for him. The book was covered with a black colored cheque leather and on which yellow italic letters reads 'ENVIRONMENTAL ENCYCLOPEDIA'

The book became his partner ever until death. He used to spend hours reading it, embroiling his young mind. Often he used to disappear from his house, come late for the lunch and sometimes even entered the house in a savage form, carrying weedy scent. Once he was scolded for going to the wilderness on his reply he said. 'Nature is my friend and I will always work for it'

During his school hours he used to disappear into his own world, just thinking about the greenery of nature. Days passed like this, after he got the book. He kind of separated himself from the world. He was fully engaged in experiencing nature's magnificent phenomenon and he himself had built a treehouse in the woods beside his house. There he used to spend most of his time learning new every day. Partly he was able to balance his school studies, though he daydreamed but was always able to over walk rest of the pupils in the class. One day the principal called his parents to school when a glass jar containing live frogs brought by Immanuel felled on the ground and the frogs jumped everywhere causing havoc. Time passed like this and day after day he was growing from an innocent child to a genius personality

CHAPTER TWO

Early Days

Today is Friday, the 28th of January; I am feeling a little sleepy as I was writing my field notes after visiting a near lake. Two months have passed since I've written my final high school exam. I am just waiting desperately for the results to come. The mist covered the woods, but I could see the red flag flattering on my tree house top. Mother has gone to the city for doing some shopping for my birthday tomorrow. I was reading the new book written by Anmol Samsuhang, titled 'Ink Of Feelings' It was a reading environment until I got distracted by a fly buzzing on the windowsill. I got up from my place and reached three to free it, but as I looked outside unexpected things happened that amused me. I saw the school peon approaching on his bike. Hurriedly I went outside to meet him, he stopped his bike and took a package from his side bag. He said 'because of the ill health of the principal, the results are being posted to the pupils'

'Holy... What happened to him'

'He is severely attacked by someone while coming from the hamlet'

'The forest area is dangerous, don't walk alone

I was stunned to hear that.

'Anyways Immanuel, congratulations you've done well

'Because of you, our school did not lose its legacy'

'Why, uncle?

'Go check the parcel, there's a surprise

He handed me the parcel and rode away saying 'The school has sent you the biggest courier to you

I hurriedly got inside and gingery passed the living room, where my father was taking a nap. I locked my room and unboxed my package. I found six things in it, my report card, my exam paper, an accolade, a cheque for one thousand dollars, a letter and a small wooden box. My mind was full of ecstasy to find these things. Above all once my breath stopped when I got to know I became the topper in my exams around the whole Matfils. I was pleased by the accolade which my school presented to me. My mind diverted to the small box which was sealed by a transparent sheath. I walked to my study table and took out a cutter from the drawer. Then I removed the cover and opened the box. I found a scroll secured with a red ribbon and again another letter, but it was from the mayor of Matfils. It reads:

Dear Immanuel Green,

Firstly, I would like to congratulate you on behalf of your high school results, and I am glad to know you are the son of Mr. David Green, who is one of my great friends. I hope you will make the name of Matfils shine more in the coming days.

I have a small gift for you to give away, which I am going to present to you on the 30th of January at the university hall, I hope you'll bring your father too. For now, I would like to inform you that I have provided a scholarship to you at the Matfils science university, if you are interested you can apply.

Mayor

Bulhort, Matfils

The former letter was from the Science university, telling me to join any department I wish. I got very happy and was not in a favor of declining it. I took the scroll and looked through it and I found it was the admission form. I jumped off my bed and ran to my father, he was in a deep sound sleep. But my excitement couldn't wait any longer, so I woke him up. Although he was in a dizzy state, he enquired me about the reason I disturbed him. I screened him the letter in front of his face. I also brought other things. As he went through the lines, was amazed. I kept looking into his face until drops of tears fell on the paper he held, there was complete silence in the room and I was in total collusion about the reason he wept. Suddenly he exclaimed 'I am proud of you son, you gave me so much happiness. He grabbed my hand, pulled me, and embraced me in his arms.

Ting! tong! Immanuel! honey!

'I am home, mom shouted outside.

Dad walked to the door and snatched all the bags, she was carrying and he banged them on the table. He rushed to me along with mom, and cried 'look sweetheart our son is great, I am so happy and you will be too'

My mother was in a confused state as she saw dad getting wild, she calmed dad and asked him everything.

'David, relax what happened?

With an excited voice, 'our son has become the topper in the high school exam for this year. Besides that, he has been given a scholarship by the mayor'

'That's amazing, a scholarship? where?

'At the Matfils Science University

As I noticed her expression had an instant change after listening to the name, anyways she said 'That's great my son

We three had a nice conversation till the sunset and it was such a lovely moment. The night spread its dark blanket. Then mother started to prepare the meal for the night and dad went to the living room for completing some of his pending work.

I went to my room, opened my computer, and surfed the internet to knowing out the Matfils university much better. And as I kept looking and reading, I jumped into a photo with four people. I examined the photo with accuracy and noticed a familiar face, the person was exactly like my father. I hurriedly connected my printer to the pc and took the photo out. I was shocked to see that the person's face and my dad's face matched, I even tried comparing it with one of his photos it was him, but filled with little doubt I opened the website on which it was posted. Initially, it reads ' History of Science in Matfils'

I gleaned through numerous pages and finally stopped on one page, I jotted the lines written on it. Finally, I found it was him, Mr. Green, and others were Dr. Cortwell, Mr. Batch, and Mr. Samson. They were the prestigious people who laid the foundation of the university. I was feeling bad that he concealed everything from me, knowing that I was going to study there. I went to the living room, but there were unknown people attending a forum. I walked back and instead went outside. It was a moonlight night, so I strolled into the lane above my house and reached the viewpoint.

CHAPTER THREE

DAD'S STORY

After I reached the viewpoint, I sat on the bench. My mind was on the rays of light arising from my house. I looked at the hills that I used to glance at during the evening time, but now it looked more beautiful when the moonlight touched the canopy. I earnestly took out my mobile and captured the glamourous moment, it felt like someone had sprinkled glitter on a black cloth. Two hours passed and I was fixed there, suddenly I sensed someone approaching, it was dad. He just came to me and sat beside me, he did not speak a word, we just sat in silence. A couple of minutes later he placed his hand on my shoulder and said 'Look my boy, never place yourself in solitude even if the biggest things happen in your life, tomorrow is your birthday and you shouldn't be here, let's go. He got up and pulled me, but I remain firm at my place. He again sat down and exclaimed ' I am sorry Immanuel I did not share anything with you, I saw you what were you doing at your table?

'So you saw the photo?

He continued 'Yes dear, and it's me, clicked way back when we founded the university.

'Dad now you'll tell me everything about that'

He nodded his head with a gloomy face.

Dark started his story, I was a brilliant boy just like you who had an avid thirst for knowledge I wanted to become a chemist and dreamed about working in pasture's institute. But I suffered a lot financially way my father and your great grandfather George Stephen Green was an alchemist and my mother I don't remember her, she died when I was born. I used to see my father doing alchemy and liked it so much that and wanted to do it by myself. Once I thought I will make an alchemist but during those days' alchemy was getting extinct, my father was the last of his kind in the whole country and was getting older and older day by day. He was working on the elixir of life which would make him immortal or increase his longevity, but he had no resources for it so he left for Africa where he could find some herbs. I was left to our neighbor's hand Mrs. Kip who raised me from when I was seven, she raised me like her own son and also send me to school at her own expense. Actually, her two children were grown up and married she used to stay alone in her house her husband was a veteran who stayed with her elder son. We stayed like a family for 10 years, but after two weeks I celebrated my 18th birthday she left us because of colon cancer. She left me a small part of her wit net worth of $50,000 in my name. In the very year, I finished high school, and one month before Mrs. Kip died, I was about to join the college but because of her sudden demise, they will force me to stop studying. Then I was left alone with new houses both filled with agony and memories which made me nostalgic. But one day I thought I have to work hard and have to stand on my feet, so I decided to start a business. First, I did some investments and started to brew wine, which I learned from my father it was a great choice and the business was exponentially getting up. Two years later I turned 20 and my pocket was full of cash, then I grew my business larger and started to supply dairy products and vegetables. Although I was rich, I did not have many academic qualifications and hadn't succeeded in my dream of becoming a chemist. So, I thought I would do something that would help someone like me achieve his or her goal. With my acquired wealth I stepped into politics and successfully became a senator in the education department. After Two years I arranged a forum at Matfils city and discussed with another businessman Mr. Batch, Mr. Sampson the lawyer, and Dr. Cortwell a biotechnologist. Then with the initiative of Mr. Sampson and the embroilment of the other three including me we were successful in founding the Matfils science university, this was one of my greatest milestones ever achieved in my life. But my life took an ugly fate and everything was destroyed on the evening of 15th December, group of policemen came to our house and arrested me by saying you've committed a murder of doctor Cortwell, I was in a dilemma and totally benumbed, thoughts started arising in my confused head, how can I do that to my colleague I wondered. And tried my best to make the policeman understand the scene but they reluctantly took me away. I was brought to the court and Mr. Sampson was fighting my case but sadly he lost and I was proved guilty, also being jailed for five years. My business was totally collapsed and everything was saturated. On 17th December after five years passed, I was released from the prison with all the hopes deaden. But on the very year I Met Your Mother at the Matfils hospital who provided me courage and lit my Jeal. on 1st may two years later I recovered my lost wealth and status, then on 27 July on the very year I got married with Victoria, your mother, it's been 25 years when I got married 30 years about the incident took place and tomorrow it will be 17 years when you were born. But don't laugh, honestly telling I am 58 years old now. Nothing till now have made me cry except the days when I kept waiting for my dad who never returned. Nevertheless, God has given me a wonderful wife and a son.

'Dear Emmanuel we must return now it's 9:00 o'clock your mother must be looking for us' dad said looking at his phone. I nodded and got up, we went down to our house, where mother was waiting for us for the dinner.

'Where you people have gone, I was worried about you two' mom said serving the food.

'We were watching the moon' dad said blinking an eye with me.

We had our dinner in silence, I got up first then washed my dishes went to my room I read some books and scrolled the Internet. A couple of minutes later I felt drowsy, so I switched off the light and when to sleep.

CHAPTER FOUR

NIGHTMARE

In the morning I woke up from my sleep and drank water sitting on my bed. For a few minutes, I was still drowsy and was still dreaming, suddenly my mind struck that today is my birthday. I became ardent about my parents and got up from the bed and stepped out. As I stepped on the ground my feet plunged into the water, I was totally obstinate by this happening then I turned the room's light revealing that the whole floor was filled with water and my focus was on the place where the flowing and splashing sound of water was coming. It was coming from the hall near the main door I hurriedly went there drawing the water with my feet. There I got totally distressed seeing the scene, in the main door, water was pummeling and squeezing through the space. I got very scared and was worried about my parents of whom

There was no clue. All the places which I investigated were vacant without my parents but full of water. Everywhere I rolled my eyes and I could only see glittering shaking of the water reflecting on the ceiling of every room which I enter.

Lastly, I decided to get out of the house as it was rapidly submerged. But I was irked by my condition, all the exits were being pumped with water, so I could not get out unless I break the main door. So, I swam to the door and tried to open it but it was locked from the outside, I was confused that who had locked it. I remember a crowbar lying on the kitchen table, and so I moved to the kitchen against the strong flowing water. As I reached the kitchen there on the window I saw that the whole place which once we had our lovely garden was completely submerged by water. Every small material there was floating in the gray water, this scene took me to the lugubrious mind which was chanting 'I am in Agony '. I was fixed at the place and my eyes were fully adhesive to the window, I could feel that the water was rising, the window plane was cracking and I would be splashed by water . my all concentration was flowing on the window , The glass plane broke open and the dozen pieces along with the strongest force of water charged me on my face . God save me save me Couple minutes later after everything was whitened in Immanuel's eyes, he finds himself alive on his bed. It revealed that it was just a disturbing nightmare, which had some meaning.

CHAPTER FIVE

BIRTHDAY

I was totally freaked out by the nightmare and was scared to get off my bed. But somehow, I managed to step out, and then I changed my outfit. I was busy folding my blankets when something busted. 'Thong'......

I grew suspicious about the sound and thought that it was another dream. So, for formality, I pinched my forearm. 'Ouch,' it was reality. I moved to the kitchen, surprisingly the lights were switched off.

'Mom... Dad.' I tried reaching them, but no response was shown. As I walked to the living room, the lights turned on, the party popper popped and all my relatives and family member jumped in, singing the birthday songs. It was a pleasant moment for me. After they finished, I thanked them and sat down. It was a sense of great happiness, that all my relatives had come for celebrating my birthday. The whole house was carrying the serenity of love. The people were uncle Jhon, the only lawyer in our family whose son was studying medicine abroad, Aunt Lily an astrologer, Aunt Sandra a baker, Aunt Molly a journalist, Uncle Fedrick a painter and oldest of all, their father, Grandpa Kurt a 107-year-old veteran who fought in the second world war. Everyone got busy with their own work, so I went to the bathroom and got refreshed. After coming out, I was shocked to see the transformation of the place. The whole house was decorated in a palatial manner and that was organized by grandpa. Mom came to me rushing, pulled me to the room and hurriedly opened the wardrobe, then handed me a plastic bag. She told me to change into those clothes. As I looked inside, I found a new black suit, I changed into it and dashed downstairs. The whole house was filled with people wishing me; a 'happy birthday.' As I could not see my family members, I started to seek them. When I moved to the hall, I found them there. The place was in an ecstasy of glittering decoration, a giant mahogany chair was placed, where I was made to sit. A couple of minutes later, everyone gathers around me and filled the hall. A birthday song was sung and a giant cake was brought to the table, I blew out the candles for my 17th birthday. I was feeling so much of happiness after a long time, perhaps it was my best birthday till now. After everything was finished the people of Bulhort were given a great feast. Our whole house and even the garden were filled with different unknown people. I was pleased with Grandpa Kurt for arranging such a big celebration. I came out of my house; I saw the workers loading food to distribute at the hamlets nearby. I was standing on a towering balcony, and as I rolled my eyes into the forest near my house, I saw something unusual. I saw a tall person creeping on the floor. He was dressed in an article of primitive clothing; he looked like an African tribesman. But because of the mist, it was not properly visible. So, I rushed to my room and got my binoculars. But as I looked, nothing was there, he was gone. I was busy looking for that creep, suddenly I was disturbed by dad.

'My boy what are you doing here, you are supposed to be inside, come let's get in.'

'Sure dad.' me hesitating.

Every guest gathered once again and started giving me gifts of different sizes and colorful wrappings. Soon the gift made a gargantuan stack, roughly sized of a school bus. After I received the last gift, uncle Jhon placed it on the stack saying 275th birthday present Ouff and sat down on the floor. The sun was biding the day off and also the guests and people went back to their place. Then I again experienced the silence of our home, all the places were vacant although my relatives were there, everyone was exhausted and got dispersed to their own world, I went to take some herbal tea, and after that, we gathered for our dinner, and everyone was in a happy state and were having a talk on today's party, after having our meal mom and aunt Sandra took the dishes and cleaned the table. Then Grandpa Kurt in a Shockey movement and a frowned face took a tiny gift He shrieked 'Young man' my grandson. It's been a very hard time for me during my teenage, and I wasn't able to live my life to the fullest, so here take it and open it. I came near him and tore through the wrapping There was a small pouch with a symbol of SUV company, I went inside the pouch and I found a car by Grandpa continued... Hehe, surprised, my boy now you are the owner of the new SUV best of luck, and once again happy birthday ...my grandson, take it a small gift of love 'thank you, grandpa, love you so much' And don't worry my son, though you are not eighteen, I have made your documents in which you are eighteen, will soon go for your license test, Dad added.... Sure dad, uncle Jhon then took a square big box and banged it on the table.

'Come here my nephew this is for you, happy birthday once again, and hope you like my present.'

I opened the box revealing that there were ten books on environment and ecology, I was so happy with these......'Thank you, uncle'

Uncle Fedrick came near me and gave me a portrait of mine, which was painted by himself...

It was so nice and perfectly made, 'Thank you, uncle'...

Aunt Sandra came and handed me a box and said... 'here you go' Immanuel 'handle her with care.'

I hurriedly opened it and a small Persian kitten jumped off it... Everyone loved it and sounded ''0hhhh'...

'Thank you, aunt I always wanted a pet, like her'...

Aunt Molly gave me a present and said 'Immanuel as you like to wander woods and forest, sometimes you want to capture, mesmerizing moments, at that time use this ...happy birthday' ...

I opened it and it was the latest model of a DSLR camera

'Thank you, aunt,' ...

Aunt Lilly took a locket out of her bag and placed it on my neck ... 'It is called the necklace of 'Tutumorota' ancient belonging to the ancient astrologer of Africa.

The necklace will protect you from animals in the wilderness and also it will give you superhuman strength in case you are in the wilderness and are in danger...she continued...

There was total confusion among everyone, Grandpa Kurt criticized and said 'Ok Lilly my daughter you've gone far now we should give his mother and father a chance' ......

"Thank you, aunt Lilly."

"You're welcome my boy," Aunt Lilly said giving me a freaking smile ...

Lastly, Mom and Dad came, they first gave me a new jungle bag which I wanted to buy for a long time,

"Are you not going to check inside it?" said...Dad.

I opened the zip and found the whole outfit for wood exploration, which are worn by professionals.

There was a hat, scouts half pant and shirt, scarf, socks, boots, half jacket and a pair of nitrile gloves.

'Thank you, mom and dad, for all this, I love you' and I hugged them.

'We will always love you too son'

I wept and said ' I love you all, thank you everyone' and started hugging everyone.

It was a memorable night and aunt molly took multiple shots. I went to my room with all my presents, I was so much elated. But I was thinking is of that tall, slender man in those African attire. From this coming Monday, I was joining the college and was thinking of the day to come. Lying on my bed with these thoughts, I fell asleep and dived into the world of dreams.

CHAPTER SIX

THE WOUNDED DEER

Immanuel was in a jovial state but also at the same time, he was feeling a kind of nervousness, as he was joining the Matfils science university. But Mr. Green's state of mind also deteriorated and struggling with the old past memories. Mrs. Green and aunt Sandra were happily preparing breakfast. Grandpa Kurt was praying, aunt lily meditating, and Uncle John and Uncle Fedrick were playing chess.

My mind was fickle but acted normal in Infront of my family. I was sitting near a window, till when aunt Lily arrived and spoke "Look son, I have got something to tell you, could I'

"Sure aunt, go on"

"Ok look, according to your birth natal, you'll come across two people in your college days with whom you'll return the glory of a foreign place"

I did not take much importance to her.

"Wow aunt that's great" and I walked away.

I was called by my mother for having breakfast. I went there after getting ready. Then with a light supper, I walked to the car and sat inside. All my family came outside to bid me accept aunt Lily who was standing near a window, looking at me. Honestly speaking I find her creepy, sometimes. But she is a very respected person around the country of Matfils, even ministers and laureates come to her, as every prediction made by her comes true, some way or the other.

A few moments later, dad came and sat beside me in our BMW. Our driver, Chups also came and sat.

The car started and left the royalist garden behind the Green

family waving them bye.

'He must be coming, so everyone, get ready' an anonymous person is seen talking to a group of people in a large decorated room.

I am still with those mixed feelings cracking in my head, but dad seems to be more intense. We were passing through a coniferous forest, and instantly after Chups slowed the car, we all stood aghast at the sudden sight of a wounded deer. It was impaled with a traditionally crafted spear; the blood was oozing and squirting in the air. We were able to predict a human attack on it. We got down the car and went near for rescuing it. It was totally benumbed and petrified.

"Who did this dastardly act, we must call the cops and the guilty will be penalized."

"You are right dad, let's call the sheriff"

"Wait these are African spears" dad exclaimed

I hurriedly googled it and yes it matched.

Meanwhile, the three were examining the deer, behind the bushes two men in tribal attire were gesticulating with each other to flee from the scene.

Dad called the sheriff, Mr. Grankful.

We saw the deer pushing its legs firmly and breathing it last.

'Sir the deer is dead! Chups cried.

'What' dad in a shocked voice.

Till then the police arrived, and as they dismounted from their vehicle, all of them were shocked to see the grim bloodshed around.

Instantly they sealed the place and forensics started their work. The sheriff came to us and said 'Sir, nowadays this way is marked in the red zone as different happening is taking place here like the attack on the principal of Bulhort high school, the missing of dogs and goats. And with few other interrogations, we continued on our way. Thirty minutes

passed and we entered the Capital of Matfils.

The Greens controlled their inconstant mind, but the more their car moved on passing streets and buildings, the more they were alarmed. Finally, after fifteen minutes, we reached the compound gate. Chups got down and went to the old gatekeeper, who had already been sleeping a long before.

He was awakened by Chups. After snapping out of his dream, he picked up his fallen cap and opened the gate. While we were passing inside, his eyes caught dad. He called dad and ran near our car. He started crying "David sir, did you recognize me, the beggar to whom you provided a job as a gatekeeper, it's me"

"Yes dear, are you doing good, and how about your daughter?

"Sir because of your help, she is now able to achieve her dream of becoming a doctor, thank you so much" the guard with folded hands and unstoppable tears.

"Look my friend, stop crying and it's all because of your hard work, I just gave you a job, all credit goes to you."

Dad took out his wallet and gave him 1000$, and waved him bye. There we were welcomed by a hostess, and she guided us to the place where we could meet the dean.

The compound is pretty big, we crossed several doors and walked across gardens and sitting areas. But the places were vacant, where are the students? I thought.

After a few minutes of walking, we reached a gigantic hall, the lady pushed the finely polished pinewood door. The door opened with a thunderous noise that echoed in the darkness of the hall.

"It's empty, ma'am" dad exclaimed

'No sir, they are here"

And the lights suddenly turned on causing thousands of people to get revealed, that the darkness had covered them.

Everyone stood up and welcomed us through musical orchestra and garlanding. The members of the science university cried 'Welcome back sir' to see one of the directors back to the college once again. We were made to sit in front together with the mayor and the dean. I met both of them and they congratulated me, whereas dad hugged them.

Different prestigious people around the world had come there for celebrating the new year. We enjoyed the cultural programs that took place. After that, the mayor felicitated a person with the golden sword award. It is given to a person of Matfils who has given their exceptional duties for the development of the country and is presented only after one decade. The golden sword award was given to nonother than dad. Dad gave an excellent speech but to the sorrowful past memories he uttered with moans at the last, perhaps he wept on the stage. Then lastly I was called upon and was presented with the highest merit award, by the mayor. After the function was over, we were taken for a joint meal with all the prosperous people from all around the globe.

Around 6 O'clock we left, thanking everyone. The dean addressed me to come on time tomorrow. While returning from the same place we'd come in the morning, I remembered the bloody scene that continued flashing in my thoughts. The accident site was sealed and the body of the deer was taken. After one hour of our departure from the function, we finally reached home. After we got down, Chups parked the car and he returned home. Then as we were about to enter, we heard aunt molly shouting inside. We ran inside, there aunt Lily and aunt molly were having a serious controversy, over the TV remote. They were quarreling for which channel to play, either astrological talks favored by aunt Lily or BBC news favored by aunt Molly. As soon as their eyes caught us, we were pulled there and both of them started to show their own complaints.

'Look, David, I was peacefully watching the predictions of baba Vanga until when Molly snatched the remote and turned on the news channel, when I told her to play the previous channel, she called me an orthodox. When I complained papa about her, he also ignored my appeal.

No one loves me.' she started to cry uncontrollably

I was shocked to see aunt Lily who was a modest and wise person to behave like that.

"Stop crying like a baby" aunt Molly again started.

"Why, you have to talk? Molly! leave her alone" Grandpa Kurt thundered.

"Papa you're in Lily's side, that's unfair"

Dad trying to mitigate the situation, wailed 'Silence'

"Everyone silent now, no one will speak"

There was a pin drop silence.

"Ok, now this seems fine"

"Everyone look, Immanuel have won the highest merit award, and I am felicitated by the Golden sword award." Dad lifting his award.

"Excellent my, nephew and grandson"

"Wow, honey! Mom took a look at both the awards

The two who were fighting earlier looked at each other and smiled.

"For celebrating the achievement of two Greens, I will prepare something special" aunt Sandra getting up and walking to the kitchen.

"I am full aunt" I said leisurely

"No, you have too anyhow"

I went to my room and got to know that mom has brought my books for the ecology course. I hurriedly checked them and found it so comprehensive. I changed my dress and thought of researching on the African spears. So, I opened my PC and went on surfing the web, in the middle I was interrupted by aunt Sandra, she called me for the dinner. I closed the computer and went to the dinning room. After having food, everyone dispersed. I went and read some books, but I felt drowsy so I went to bed.

CHAPTER SEVEN

JOINING COLLEGE

I could hear the alarm clock ringing and I could see the shimmering rays of the sun falling on the gable, which made me realize it was already 9 O'clock. As I walked towards the bathroom, I smelled a fusty odor coming from aunt Lily's room. Though it was bad, I peeped inside her room through the keyhole, she was burning incense and was meditating. In the hall, Grandpa Kurt was praying. Mom saw me moving around in an idle manner "Immanuel get ready fast, you've to leave at 10, for your class."

I went to the bathroom took a shower, changed my clothes, and went for my breakfast. After my meal, I got in my SUV with Chups. After fifty minutes, we reached our destination.

"Hey Chups, now to get me you can around in four in the evening to bring me"

"Sure sir, as you say" and he drives back.

With a deep breath and constant esteem, I stepped into the compound. To my surprise, I was five minutes early, which made me more confident to face others. Early morning I was greeted by the old gatekeeper. I walked to the ecology block where I found my classroom. I was the last to arrive, as I entered the class there were many new faces staring at me, I silently walked and sat beside a boy named Charles. After a couple of minutes later the dean along with four other professors walked in. Everyone got up from their seat, and again we sat back with the order of the dean.

"Good morning, dear students, Prof. Harvey Saints, the dean of the university, welcome you all in session. In this place, you will unrip the secrets of ecology and will be guided by these four prominent professors. I introduce them now, Dr. Evangelista, Dr. Simpson, Dr. Jhon and Dr. Montgomery, they are skilled professors having an experience of over 27 years. After you all graduate from here, you all will ripe the fruit of knowledge in ecological sciences and will definitely do something groundbreaking in the future. Now we will leave on to Prof. Jhon to take his first class. Enjoy your day students" then he walked away.

The professor started teaching us, but I was busy observing other chaps around. I could see there were mostly Matfilians, but in small numbers, there were students from other countries too. The first day at college was good, I made friends with Charles, my desk partner. He is inquisitive, charming, and a little talkative. He is actually from England but had migrated to Matfils. From this day, he became my full-time best friend at the college.

Just like this my college days also passed away in no time. Everything was fine until something unusual happened one day. In our class, there was a boy from Tanzania named Kofi, who remained mostly silent, gentle, and calm. He did not talk much to everyone in the class and used to come early and leave early. For his introverted behavior, he was given the epithet of 'Lone owl.' Nothing was wrong with him until, one evening, when Chups texted me that he wouldn't be able to pick me up, because of toothache. So I had to go on walking, the most disturbing thing was the sun was setting and I still had to cross the dense forest path. But with a bold heart, I took my way. In the dark floor of the forest, every step raked and echoed. I walked faster and faster, trying to boost my agility. After fifty minutes of walking, I entered the middle hamlets of western Matfils. There was a soiree around a campfire which was having a discussion on seeing a tribal person on the way to Bulhort. I went thinking about hearing the news and walked faster. Miles away from the hamlet, in the forest path, I saw an unexpected thing. Kofi my classmate was walking into the wilderness, of nowhere. I was shocked to see him amidst the forest and not only that he was going in the reserved forest zone. I tried following him until my body started to stagger, suddenly. Unbelievable! the locket of Tutumorota, started to glow green, which controlled my body to run away from the place. Soon, I lost Kofi and he somewhere disappeared into the woods.

After a lengthy walk, I finally reached home and it was already dusk. Everyone in the house was shocked to see me coming at this time.

"What happened to you, Immanuel? You're two hours late."

"Actually mom, today Chups was not able to come because of toothache"

"What? He didn't come, are you alright then, the forest area is not safe these days"

"I am totally fine"

"But look, son, it's dangerous to walk through the silent forest road alone" aunt Sandra added

"Sandra, don't be silly he is a grown-up man and above all, he has the Tutumorota" aunt Lily with a smile

"It's better to keep your doctrine away, Lily my sister" Uncle Fedrick spoke

I felt irritated and shouted "OK, is everyone done with their philosophies, I am fine, nothing has happened to me. I just walked past a forest, that's it, don't exaggerate"

I left and went to my room for changing. I was thinking about Kofi, suddenly an idea stroked in my head, maybe Aunt Lily can help. I ran to her room, it was locked from the inside, so I knocked. She opened and I spoke to her "Aunt I need your help"

"Come in nephew"

I sat on the sofa, opposite her.

"So, what is your problem"

"This evening, when I was coming across the mid forest, I saw my friend walking into the wilderness. Then I tried following him until the Tutumorota started glowing green, and with that, my body became involuntary bringing me back home."

She shrieked "Immanuel, the locket which you are wearing belongs to your grandpa and is our family heritage, but only Grandpa Kurt knows how it came to us. It was made by an astrologer, long ago in Africa, and is fully enchanted. If you trust it will definitely save you any cost. The green illumination indicates danger, that's why it protected you, you trusted it earlier, son"

"Look nephew, I will spread this deck of tarot cards and with a pure devotion, pick one"

"OK, anyone?

"Yes, go on"

"I will go for this"

"Oh, the majestic one! It says that you are destined to fulfill a great work, you are chosen by God, don't disappoint the God"

I walked out carrying a dizzy mind. After our dinner, without doing anything I landed on my bed it felt like I died, as I was very tired.

CHAPTER EIGHT

DEATH OF GRANDPA

Two and half years later.

We all are seated with the Dean, posing for the graduation photo. I don't know how the three years passed so fast.

I am very happy today as we all have received our B.Sc. degree in ecological science. It was given by the hands of Dr. Teshercov, an educationist. I also decided to do my master's degree studies at Matfils Science University, as I was not in a favor of leaving my friends and the college.

One month later everyone gathered for admission. Then we started attending our class as usual, through this course we also went to different places for excursions. Like the largest delta Sundarbans, Yellowstone national park, and Fraser Island. With all our embroilment, after two years of joining college, once again we all gathered for another picture of receiving the M.Sc. degree. After the photo session was over, everyone was busy gulping the feast. Till then the dean came to me and asked "So, Immanuel are you thinking to click another picture with us for our doctoral studies."

I humbly replied, “That would have been great sir, but I am thinking of going abroad for my higher education.”

“That’s great to hear, but of course, we would feel heavy to lose such a shining student”

I smiled back in return.

“Anyways it was our fortune to have you here for five years, we already had the privilege of keeping you, go and study where you want, you will always remain in our hearts, many blessings from my side” lifting his hands.

“Thank you, sir, for everything which you provided me, I gained immense knowledge here, with the professors, and the university and you will always remain in my heart.

Then I returned home feeling nostalgic about the first time I joined the college. I was driving the car when I reached the place where five years before, and we saw the wounded deer. I stopped the car, got down, and walked around. It also reminded me of Kofi, he had left the college after his bachelor’s studies. I had not told Charles that I am going abroad, but he had told me that he will join the army. It started to drizzle, I ran to my car and started it. Suddenly my phone started ringing thunderously as I checked it there was an incoming call from aunt Molly. I received it.

“Immanuel! Son where ever you are please come here, Grandpa’s health is deteriorating, and he wants to meet you. Don’t go back home, mom and dad are already here”

Aunt whimpering.

Speaking about Grandpa he stepped at the remarkable age of 111, similar to the polish supercentenarian, Alexander Imich who recently passed. He is now the certified oldest male alive by the gunnies book of world records.

To start the car when I touched the keys in the ignition, it reminded me of Grandpa Kurt. Though he was my grandfather's youngest brother out of seven, he was like my own Grandpa. I turned the car towards Matfils and drove to the same road on which I came. After twenty minutes I reached the capital of Matfils and then at the intersection, I took the road taking me to the eastern part of the Matfils archipelago. With full winding agility, I reached the destination, in one and a half hours when it usually used to take three hours.

Outside the house I could see our BMW and Uncle Jhon's Ferrari, parked. I got down my car and went inside, I directly walked to Grandpa's room. There everyone had gathered around Grandpa. Everyone was silent, I walked near him and sat beside him.

I such a senility, he spoke to me "My grandson, you've finally arrived at my deathbed, I was waiting long for you to come and get finally eluded in nature" Laughing.

I literally cried after seeing him speak like that.

"Hey young man, don't cry for a 111-year-old senile person, it's already time for passing the record to another supercentenarian,"

"But I love you and I want you to be with us for more years"

"Who lives to eternity, I am not an Alchemist like you Grandfather, and birth and death are the laws of nature, you can't forbid it, be happy and accept what is happening"

Everyone around started to cry and moan.

"I have lived my life to the fullest and now I have become obsolete and senile. Before I leave, I would like to give you a task and your work is to complete it. Will you do it for me? Promise me..."

"I will surely accomplish it; I promise to fulfill your dream"

"Lily! In my wardrobe there is a big key, maybe inside my uniform, bring it to me"

Aunt Lily hurriedly looked for the key and found it, after that she handed the large rusted key to me.

"Listen, Immanuel, this is the key to the secret bunker which I made during the war, it is located in the ravine beside the old hamlet. But, mysteriously summons only in five years, this year it would have been formed but it's too late, don't miss the next opportunity. It will form on the wall of the ravine on one side, get inside you'll come to know everything"

"Now to my family, I would like to thank each one of you for taking care of me. Till now I have no regrets, to leave, I worked hard, lived in riches, ate luscious foods, and have stayed healthy, I am happy and am free to die"

He closed his eyes and we all noticed his long, deep breath until he stopped breathing. Everyone around started to cry loudly and I could see Aunt Sandra crying the most. I fell into the sea when the main pillar of the family collapsed. Aunt Sandra came near him and saluted him saying "you were a great dad."

The funeral was to take place tomorrow, and soon the journalists and the media arrived spreading the news of the death of the oldest person. All of us slept with hearts full of agony.

Tomorrow it was decided to bury the corpse at the military graveyard. It was a sorrowful moment and the funeral was concluded in the afternoon. With this, the story of Col. Kurt Green, the last World War 2 veteran of Matfils and the oldest person in the world ended.

One week later, we all were back in our daily life. My passport was ready for going abroad, it was couriered to me.

I told dad about joining the research institute form next month which is in England. I had done my admission there and have finished booking a ticket for the plane. I was leaving two days later and started to get prepared right from that day.

Today I had to leave for England, everyone have once gathered to meet me. Dad, Mom, Uncle Jhon, Aunt Lily, Uncle Fedrick, Aunt Molly and Chups went to me till the airport. Then said bye to everyone and told them to see after five years. After my registration and checking, I left my luggage to get on the plane. While getting in the plane, I looked back and waved my family. I could not say how much upset I was to leave Matfils, tears were flowing from my eyes. After getting on board, I got the seat near the window and after waiting for thirty minutes the plane took off.

In about nineteen minutes, we reached Russia and from there I again got in another plane, taking me to England.

Then about ten hours later, the plane reached England. After getting down and collecting my things, I called uncle Fedrick's brother-in-law, Jackson, to get me. I waited for 10 minutes and then he arrived with a cab. Then I, got in the vehicle and was feeling the wind of England and there in the car, 500 hundred miles was playing, which reminded of my home. After a drive of half an hour, we reached our destination. There, I was given a separate flat for rent and indeed it was in a great condition. It took me one whole month to fill the place. On that day I had my dinner upstairs at Jackson's apartment.

Next day I got up around in six in the morning, went to the bathroom and got refreshed. I had my breakfast, got dressed up and around 10, I left for my class. There at the institute, I was the first to come and couple of minutes later the junior researchers started coming. My overall routine during my doctoral program. Everything in my PhD course went smoothly, without any hindrances.

CHAPTER NINE

Political Instability

Today is a prosperous day for me as today we will be getting our Ph.D. degree, at the hands of the director. It was a memorable day for all the researchers. After the ceremony, together with my batchmates, I had a tour of the city of London. We went to see big ben and sailed on the Thames. In the evening as soon as I reached my apartment, I had to pack my things up as I was returning to Matfils, tomorrow.

I woke up early morning and called mom on the telephone. She warned me about the situation of Matfils and told me to call immediately after reaching there. I was dropped off at the airport by Jackson and got on board. In one day and one night, I reached Matfils during the evening. I changed my sim card and phoned Mom. She told me that Chups was on his way to bring me. I waited for seven minutes and he arrived. I got inside the car and spoke to him.

"Hey brother, how are you doing?

"Fine sir, and need to tell you, good news"

"Sure, tell me"

"I had my marriage done two weeks earlier"

"Wow! Great to hear, I wished to be there"

"She is a doctor"

"Great to hear, congratulations"

"Thank you, sir,"

"Mom was talking about some political instability"

"Yes sir, the son of Anthony Denver is now the President of Matfils, nothing worst can be like that"

"What? Is that true"

"Totally true sir, but not only that the people are violently uprising against the new rules made by him. He is also encroaching on the forest areas nearby for extracting the resources."

"Oh no! that seems very bad"

As we entered Matfils city, I was stunned to see the destruction around. A riot was approaching us, so Chups flew the car from there. The shops were destroyed, governmental buildings mutilated and parks burnt. The worst to see was the statue of the founders, including dad, which stood in front of our university collapsed. I felt the worst experience ever in Matfils. This was the because of the felonious Denver. Within one hour we reached home.

There Mom and Dad were waiting eagerly for me to come, as I stepped out there was a sudden change in their expression. I ran to them and hugged them. Then we got to our house.

But besides the bad news, I got to hear a sudden shocking news. Our dad had become the new mayor of Matfils but was being suppressed by Denver. After discussing the new topics, we had our dinner and I restlessly landed on my cozy bed, after five years. I woke up at midnight and by some kind of noise. I felt like a piece of metal being dropped on the floor. I got up and tracked the sound, following it. I came to the main hall where I saw something horrific. My spirit left no place after seeing the ghost of our Grandpa, he was constantly dropping the large key on the floor. As he saw me, in an offensive manner he rushed towards me. But to my surprise I was lying on my bed, revealing it as a lucid dream. I thanked God for saving me again. Now I realized, that I was yet to accomplish my goal, given by Grandpa. I got down from my bed, got refreshed, and walked downstairs. Their dad was bickering with a man in a black suit.

I enquired "What's the problem dad?

"Nothing, just having some official discussions"

"I don't think, you need to squabble for having a discussion"

I left them and walked to the kitchen for getting something to eat. Mom was sitting at the dining table and was busy watching YouTube videos. On the table, I saw an envelope resting. Pouring water into my cup, I asked her " Mom, what is that"

"Yes, sweetheart! Did you call me"

"What is in that envelope" me drinking water.

"Oh, how could I forget it, this is a calling letter for your appointment" with a smile.

I squirted the water as soon as I heard that.

"Appointment? Where?

"Where does an ecologist work? At the forest, I have appealed for the officer rank."

"How can you do that, that's unfair. I was thinking to go abroad for teaching at a university"

"Now forget about it, I got this reservation from the former mayor, before his resigning"

"But! I could"

"Stop, Immanuel"

"Ok, as you say"

I had cornflakes and milk for my breakfast. Mom went to the city for her usual work. After that, I cleaned the dishes and thought of seeking the secret bunker, which ought to get out this year.

A few minutes later, I changed into my ecologist outfit and took out the key from a secret vault that I had kept, five years ago. I dashed downstairs and dad caught me who was reading the newspaper.

"Hey there! Is Dr. Green going somewhere? Dad taunting

"Yes Mr. Mayor, I have some work"

We both laughed uncontrollably looking at each other.

"Immanuel, be sure to come fast"

"Sure dad"

I came outside and took the forest path behind my house. I was walking with different thoughts until I approached my treehouse. The place reminded me of my teenage days, suddenly I went to the flashback, recalling the day when I had kept a small keychain, which was gifted to me by Charles. To get that I tried putting my leg on the ladder, but the hewn wood broke out. But I was not forsaking it. So, I climbed the tree branches and finally got up to the tree house floor. There I found my old clothing, books and my box where I'd kept the thing. As I opened it, a mist of dust flew. I took out the keychain, and with it, I also found my best book "ENVIRONMENTAL ENCYCLOPEDIA." Seeing it, I felt like crying. The keychain was a small model of the great scientist Charles Darwin, my friend Charles used to say "whenever you see Charles Darwin, you have to remember me" At that time, I missed him.

Because of the dust, my nose became sniffy and I sneezed thunderously which also made me fall down. The old wood soon broke open and I fell down from a height of 20 feet.

"Ah! God! It hurts!

"Huh? it does not hurt, not a little!

I was surprised that I felt no pain, even after falling from such a height. After I got up and started to collect my fallen articles, I noticed my locked 'Tutumorota' glowing green.

It was the second time, it glowed. From now, I really started to believe in it. I said to myself "You adamant, does anyone fall after sneezing" I laughed.

I continued to my path and came to a hanging bridge, and on the other side, the ravine was present. I captured the scene from the hanging bridge and reached the other side. A few miles further, I entered a hamlet and I was like "Oh my God"

All the houses were mutilated, dead cattle, and a few people were loading their property on the back of donkeys and mules. The crops were burnt, tanks were destroyed and the floor was smeared with blood. I tried talking to some people but they seemed still traumatized. Finally, I walked near an ISKCON monk who was meditating under a tree.

"Pardon me, your holiness, can I ask what happened here?

"Nothing more than an increase in the greed of people, the village was attacked"

"Attack! Who were them."

"I am just a pilgrim from India, and I have come here to distribute the Bhagavat Gita. I arrived here, yesterday and today morning, ten bullies came here and destroyed everything. They even killed some of the people. I know that much, you can ask that old lady, she is very kind."

I walked to the lady and asked her about everything, in reply she said "Denver! He did this all, for his greed of extracting the bauxite from here, he encroached on our lands, and now the place needs to be vacant till tomorrow."

I could not do anything except leave them. I directly walked out of the hamlet and headed towards the ravine.

There on the wall, on my side, I saw a steel staircase as told by Grandpa. I went there and walked on it, leading me inward of the ravine. The level below the ground, I ended up in a dark tunnel. As I could not see anything, I turned my flashlight on and walked inside. There, I approached a giant iron door and beside it, there was a switch. I pressed the switch and the whole tunnel lit up. I noticed a keyhole, so I took the key and put it there. The door opened and I happily got in. The interior was beautifully designed, a monitor was placed there and a remote was lying on a table, there was also a paper note in which it was written 'Turn on.' As I turned it on, Grandpa Kurt appeared on the screen. He started to talk

"Hello,

I Col. Kurt Green, on behalf of my 90th birthday shoot this video to convey the unknown past. Fifty years have passed since I made this bunker, during the second world war. And after fifty years I have again come here on my 90th birthday to show the secrets which are trapped in the wilderness. One year before the second world war broke out, a wicked mayor ruled Bulhort. He was Anthony Denver, who went to went Kenya, for looting the natural resources including the horn of the white rhino. To this, the tribal Maasai people of that area roused into flames. They fearlessly fought with the henchmen of Denver with their traditional weapons, until they perished to the last man. Few of them managed to flee into the wilderness. Even the sacred statue of their deity, Enkai was lifted by those attackers. Not only that, they even abducted ten Maasai children for experimentation by a mad scientist named Dr. Thomas. Who had been hired by Denver to collect the rare species and resources? When the loot reached Matfils, their was a total political instability. The valuable materials did not get sold, because of the situation. The children were thrown to the basement at Dr. Thomas's house. They were kept in the darkness and were fed only once in a day. Two weeks later a riot broke out and it targeted Dr. Thomas for child abduction. Every time he was saved by Denver but this time, he was skinned alive by the public. With this the Maasai children ran fled away. No one knows what happened to them. A young man among the attackers at Kenya, who had a good relation with the Greens,

told that Mr. George Green was alive at Kenya and with him we got the magical locket of Tutumorota. And who ever the locket choses among the Greens, he/she is destined to return the statue back to Kenya"

With this the screen switched off. I was left with my mouth open. As I turned back, I was shocked.

CHAPTER TEN

INTO THE WILDERNESS

It was none other than Kofi, I was frozen in my place.

"Hello, old friend, nice to meet you after a gap of seven years." He spoke.

"Kofi, how come you are here, and where did you go after graduation?

"I did not come here, I was sent by your grandfather, G.S. Green."

"And it may sound unbelievable, but I am also a Maasai."

"What? are you from Kenya, and is my grandfather really alive"

"Yes, your grandpa is now 125 years old, but because of his divine powers, he is still young"

"I can't believe..."

"So will you help me in taking back our heritage, the statue of Enkai?"

"Yes, of course, Kofi it's not only your mission but mine too."

"So tomorrow, first we need to rescue our friends"

"Friends? Who."

"The ten runaway Maasais are alive, in the forest of Bulhort."

I was shocked at his reply. We came out of the bunker and exchanged our phone numbers. Then we decided to meet tomorrow. When I reached home, it was already sunset. I got in, and there mom and dad were having tea. I walked near them and opened up about my mission, I was also told I would go to Kenya.

"Kenya? But dear you have an appointment tomorrow."

"Sorry mom, this time I am not looking into any excuses. Let me go, please."

"Hesitantly, they allowed me."

Then I went to my room and started packing. I did not tell mom and dad about Grandpa George, because it might be false. Today I went to sleep early, as I needed to wake up early as possible.

I got up around five in the morning and called Kofi, he was already at the spot. Then left after a light meal, saying bye to mom and dad. I took the forest path, as we need to enter the reserved forest. Yesterday Kofi was talking about, bringing someone special. I was eager to see him. In one hour I reached there, and Kofi was in an army uniform.

I asked him, "Did you join military?

"Yup, I had already been to the army after my graduation, don't you want to meet another army man."

"Who?

"Hello, buddy are you alright?

An unexpected person, Charles walked out from behind a tree. I was soon filled with ecstasy and excitement. I ran there and hugged him tightly.

"Where were you gone, after college, no calls and texts, your phone was even switched off."

"Actually, I had gone to England for my doctoral studies."

"What? you would have told me anyways."

"Ok, guys now get to work." Kofi opened a chart.

He hung the chart to a tree and started to make us understand "Look here properly, I have a great strategy. First, we will evacuate the Maasai from the forest, then we need to do an attack on Denver's house when he is out of the home. Then take out the statue and get on the helicopter."

"And lieutenant, how are we going to attack, where dozens of guards reside and CCTV works throughout the year, you're talking about attacking in a president's house," Charles said.

"I already have arranged that, my friend works there as a chief, he will mix sleeping medications in the food and will serve to the guards. Then he will turn the CCTVs off and he himself has arranged a mob, along with the media who will reveal the dark side of Mr. President. Captain, then you have to get our helicopter so we can flee to the Matfils seaport. "

"Great strategy, a friend let's get moving." I got up.

"Wait, Kofi why these big bags? Charles asked.

"Oh! These are clothes for my people so that they won't be recognized."

We started our journey and sorrowfully passed the hamlet, which was already abandoned by yesterday. In twenty minutes, we reached the check post. There I verified and ID and registered three cards for us. One of the wildlife biologists asked me "Excuse me, Dr. Green, who are this army personnel."

"Oh, they are my friends."

"Sir, please make sure they won't use their guns, you know the rules properly. And you need to be out around three in the evening."

"Sure."

We stepped inside the compound from which the reserved forest started. After a long walk, miles inside we came across a creek, where I filled my bottle. Charles then shouted, "Guys come here." He was pointing to the ground, where a large fresh footprint of a tiger was made. We all looked at each other, then heard a roaring sound.

Charles cried "We are dead now, friends any last wishes."

Kofi said, running "To get alive."

Then in our front, a jaguar jumped Infront of us.

"Hey, it's not a tiger."

"I am not a scientist, ask Immanuel."

"It's a jaguar and you two, both have studied ecology, how could you say that."

The animal with the strongest bite was moving near us and our spirit left no place. We all closed our eyes and prayed to God. Surprisingly it turned away and ran as if it was scared by something. I saw the locket Tutumorota glowing red this time. Seeing it Kofi kneeled down and bowed to me. I told him to get up. Charles was stunned to see everything, he was confused. Few steps before we reached the small habituated area. The tribals became very happy to see us coming there.

When I stepped there my locket started to glow black, and again the Maasai people bowed to me, I felt like a God. Then we helped the tribals to dress up like us. Though they spoke in different lingua franca, the language of love was clear. They instantly became friends with us. They were Mosi, Amadi, Omari, Kojo, Davu, Nala, Amara, Juma, Zuri, and Suri. Six boys and four girls, the oldest was Omari aged 34 and the youngest was Zuri aged 18. Although they were lagging behind to leave the place where they spend their childhood, Kofi consoled them and made them walk. Kofi told me that the path they were walking was indeed dangerous, so we checked our soles. It was a tall cliff, from where we could see the beautiful Bulhort. We carefully, walked stepping on the slippery rocks, and passed the place holding the vines. It was about noon when we reached the road. I and Charles were surprised to reach the main road of Bulhort.

"This way was not discovered."

"My brothers and sister made a route for them."

"Where are we going now."

"Now I and Immanuel along with my people will go to raid Denver's residence and Captain Charles will bring our helicopter there."

"OK, let's get moving."

After we reached there, the mobile network came back. So, Kofi called the chief. He told us to get there quickly because he had already given them food. We swiftly walked to Denver's residency, and surprisingly found the guards in a deep sleep. We got in the house and everyone got dispersed looking for the statue. Then the chief arrived there, he told us to look it in the bunker. But to get access over there we needed to pick the right book from the shelf, and if we pick the wrong book a message will be sent to Denver. So, I worked my mind to examine the whole bookshelf. There I suspected a book titled 'African history' it looked a bit cleaned than the other dusted ones. With this, I decided to pull it and I was surprised to find it opening. The whole shelf opened into a chamber with stairs leading downstairs. As we walked the lights, automatically glowed. There were thousands of valuable items, which were all raid by Anthony Denver. We found our statue, in a glass seal. We took it out, it was approximately three feet tall and was made with stone carving, dating back to, maybe 900 years. There was a bug suitcase where we put the statue. Kofi told me to carry it because the person wearing the Tutumorota, could easily lift it. Then we got upstairs and gathered everyone and waited for the helicopter. After two minutes Charles arrived and he brought the helicopter in the parking area. Everyone got in and the chief had already brought the mob and media to expose the dark factory of Denver, seeing this he will be made to resign.

We were in halfway to the port and the Maasai friends seemed totally scared of the height, Zuri even vomited.

After reaching the sea port we landed in a playground. The helicopter was taken by another soldier. Me and Charles secretly got inside a cargo ship by bribing the security guards. Other including Kofi, dressed as labors and got on the ship by carrying one sack of load each. The ship took off in half an hour, which was leading to Zanzibar at Tanzania. As my sim card would work only up to few more distance, I decided to call mom and dad. But they didn't receive the call, so I rather left a voicemail. Soon, the sun started setting. It was a magnificent moment to see. I opened the small window and captured the moment with my camera. As I was feeling restless, I laid down, made the pillow on the suitcase and slept empty stomach.

CHAPTER ELEVEN

MATFILS TO AFRICA

In a dreamy world, I could hear, the cry of a bird, probably a seagull. I found myself in the same place with Charles around big oil barrels. I got up and walked around, from the window I saw the blue waters of the ocean and the cotton-like clouds hovering above. I looked in my GPS device and found that we were sailing in the Indian ocean. And I remembered the anticipation of a sea voyage to Spain where the wind was like a whetted knife. My stomach was feeling empty so, went near Charles and woke him up. I asked him something to eat, he told me there is a chocolate bar in his bag. I hungrily rushed and took the chocolate out, and took the fun of eating it. I shared it with Charles, We spend the whole day talking with each other about the past days, playing games, and laughing around.

In the evening, Kofi had come to meet us. He informed me that by tomorrow, we will reach Tanzania, and from there we will be picked up by his brother. He gave us two packets of biscuits and a bottle of hot water. He informed me that others were seriously suffering from sea fever and he was having a bad time in handling them. We slept around seven in the evening.

In the morning I could hear the blasting sound of the foghorns, irritating my ears. Through the window, I was able to see the land. I excitedly woke up Charles, and to his surprise, he asked me the reason. I pointed out towards the window, he was also very happy to see the coast. After around ten minutes we reached the Zanzibar port. This time as we were sneaking to get out, the captain approached us. The only thing we could do was to bribe him too, we left him smiling with 1000$. We got down with the suitcase and waited for others at the dockyard. After they gathered, we walked a few miles away and reached a garage. There we met Kofi's cousin, who would take us to the Maasai village. Everyone got on the bus and we drove away. I was very happy to meet Grandpa, but the Maasai seemed happier to come back to their birthplace after 2 decades. After five hours, we reached the savanna where we were dropped down. Then after two hours of walking, we could see the tiny mud huts. I could sense the happiness in every Maasais, ultimately ran to reach their home. Seeing this, I realized the difference between growing up alone with luxury and growing up with the whole village as a single family. My wealth is incomparable with the compassion in these people for each other. I and Charles were soon surrounded by a staring tribe. Then the witch doctor or Laibon, who was Kofi's grandfather, came near us and spoke something in maa language. Kofi said that he was saying thank you. Then he placed two bronze totems on my forehead, uttering some words. Then I dived into a void, where things whitened for a second. I felt like in a celestial world. Showing me the past movies of the ancient astrologer making the Tutumorota and at last, he speaks "Immanuel you have come."

Then I came back to reality, where all the tribals were on my feet. I told Kofi to get them up. Then they happily carried me and I carried the statue. I got down myself and was directed to go into a nearby dried lake and place the statue in the middle. The whole village followed me to the lake, which was dried up by drought. I got down inside, whereas the others watched from the cliff of the lake. I walked to the middle and found a beautiful ceramic structure, there a hollow place was present. I took the statue of Enkai and placed it there. And magically a beam of light rose from the statue into the sky. Soon the nimbus clouds gathered overhead and started dropping raindrops. The whole village was so much elated by the rain and started dancing there. The whole lake mysteriously filled up and I swam to the land. Then as I stepped on the soil, it instantly grew green lush grasses everywhere, making the withered plant and naked trees green again.

Every one of the Maasai tribe kneeled down to me and to my surprise found the color of the lake. Initially, it formed a whirlpool then divided into two semi-circles with black on one side and red on one side. Kofi explained to me, it was their deity showing up. The black was called the Enkai-Narok who was benevolent and the red was called Enkai-Nyokie who was vengeful. Then the Laibon started to invoke God, raising the two totems one of the oodo-mongi the red cow, and the other of oodo-kiteng the black cow. Then the black cow totem glowed black, making the lake black which indicated the end of bad days and will be replaced by happiness.

After the ritual, the villagers took us happily for a feast. Till then, I asked Kofi about Grandpa George. To this he went to his Mother, and came back saying "I am sorry, but, one week ago he left for India."

"What India? Charles shockingly.

"No problem, then I am going to India."

"I am there with you."

"You help us return our, heritage, I will help you to bring back your heritage."

"We are coming, INDIA."

Author's Note

Anmol Rai Samsuhang

The first volume of Matfils diaries is published and in the second volume there will be the story of Immanuel's grandfather, the alchemist in the next book titled 'Finding eternity'.

To find George Stephen Green, the three travel to India, experiencing a different cool vibe and lastly finding their grandpa at the ripe age of 126.

Wait for the next publications, readers!

9 798889 758846

Printed by Libri Plureos GmbH in Hamburg,
Germany